Mrs R
bow
by Neil Griffiths
Illustrated by
Judith Blake

This book was inspired by Jenny Rainbow and is dedicated to the memory of my Mum, a lovely lady who brought a rainbow into many people's lives.

Red Robin Books is an imprint of Corner To Learn Limited

Published by
Corner To Learn Limited
Willow Cottage • 26 Purton Stoke
Swindon • Wiltshire SN5 4JF • UK

ISBN 0-9545353-7-5

First published in the UK 2000
New edition published in the UK 2005

Design by
David Rose

Printed by
Tien Wah Press Pte. Ltd., Singapore

This is the house where
Mrs Rainbow lives.
Just wait until you see
what it's like inside!

She has painted the kitchen bright green, the conservatory a warm orange and the sitting room soothing shades of yellow.

Upstairs, the bathroom is ocean blue, the study a welcoming red and the guest room a restful violet. Mrs Rainbow's own bedroom, however, is decorated in one of her favourite colours, indigo and there you will find every shade of purple imaginable!

Mrs Rainbow is never happier than when relaxing in her garden. Here she is now, sitting in her favourite spot enjoying a glass of cool lemonade.

She loves her garden at all times of the year,

with the reds, golds and browns of autumn,

the silvers and whites of winter

and the yellows, purples and greens of spring ...

... but summer is Mrs Rainbow's favourite season
and today her garden looks at its best.

However, Mrs Rainbow can't relax for too long today as the village school is holding a car-boot sale and she is keen to get there early to pick up some bargains.

She is first to arrive and can hardly wait to get started. Nothing excites Mrs Rainbow more than the thought of finding something unexpected to add to her colourful home.

After an hour's hunting, she emerges smiling from the school playground clutching a burgundy patchwork cushion for the study, a bright orange candle for the conservatory, a purple mug for her night-time hot chocolate drink and a turquoise soap dish. She will have to decide later whether this will be for the bathroom or the kitchen.

On her way home, the sky begins to cloud over and a light drizzle begins to fall. By the time she reaches the house, it has turned into a very grey day indeed and Mrs Rainbow is glad to get inside.

On days like this, Mrs Rainbow usually keeps busy, working on her latest painting …

… or putting the finishing touches to a tapestry.

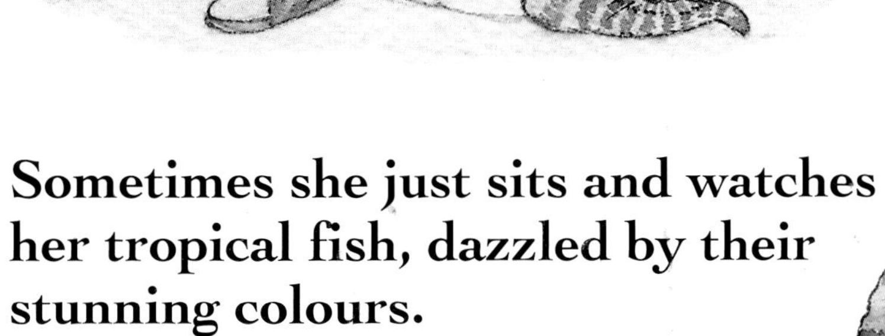

Sometimes she just sits and watches her tropical fish, dazzled by their stunning colours.

Today is different. Mrs Rainbow has hardly got her coat off before she rushes upstairs to try out the new hair colour she has bought from the chemist.

The bottle says "Bermuda Blonde" but, as she emerges from the wash basin, blonde it certainly is not. It is more like peacock green! "Perfect," thinks Mrs Rainbow as she admires herself in the bathroom mirror.

She has barely finished drying her hair when there is a loud knock at the front door.

She is greeted by three somewhat startled members of the District Council Planning Department, shocked perhaps by the colour of Mrs Rainbow's hair or by her matching outfit!

"G-g-good afternoon, madam," stutters a stout gentleman wearing a black pin-stripe suit and a bowler hat.

He explains that they are from the Planning Department and hands a letter to Mrs Rainbow to read.

The District Council
Planning Office,
Greyfriars Road,
Blackford.
Co. Dullham.

To the occupant of 'Rainbow Cottage'.
At our recent monthly planning meeting, it was decided that your house, 'Rainbow Cottage', is not in keeping with the rest of the village.

It was agreed that the cottage is far too colourful and must be immediately painted grey to match all the other buildings.

Signed: The District Council
Planning Committee

Mrs Rainbow tries to protest, as she loves her little cottage and thought everybody else did. But the councillors will not change their decision and say they are sorry, but rules are rules and the painters will start work in the morning.

As they leave, Mrs Rainbow
looks sadly at the houses
in the village beyond …

… before removing
her house sign and
gently closing
the door
behind her.

As promised, the painters arrive promptly the following morning and quickly set to work. They too feel sad, but are only following the Council's orders. Mrs Rainbow is nowhere to be seen and the curtains to the cottage remain strangely drawn all day.

News quickly spreads to the other villagers through Mrs Braithwaite, who almost rides her bicycle off the road and through the hedge when she catches sight of the newly painted cottage.

Soon, a large, inquisitive crowd of people gather outside, hardly able to believe their eyes.

It is the Reverend Fowler who finally plucks up enough courage to knock on the door and ask Mrs Rainbow how she is feeling.

After some time, she appears, looking pale and grey. She thanks the villagers for their concern and says that she is feeling a little off colour today, before returning into the darkness of the cottage.

The worried villagers hurry to the Village Hall, where a special meeting has been called to discuss the situation.

Several hours later, they emerge looking very pleased with themselves.

Early the next morning, even before the sun has risen, a long queue has formed outside Fred Stanley's DIY Store. It seems as if the whole village is there.

The following day, the Reverend Fowler, accompanied by a large crowd, arrives outside Mrs Rainbow's cottage. He knocks on the door and asks her to step out into the front garden, since they have a surprise which will bring the colour back into her life.

Mrs Rainbow, still looking pale and grey, shuffles nervously out of the doorway and stands in silent amazement. She can hardly believe her eyes!

The Reverend Fowler has painted the Vicarage purple and plum, whilst the Post Office is a startling scarlet! Jean's Hair Salon is now pastel shades of lilac and peach, the Crossroads Café a rich maroon and the Library emerald green.

In fact, every house and building in the village has been newly painted in the most glorious colours – even the church has a bright, new, yellow steeple!

Tears stream down Mrs Rainbow's face. She has never seen anything so beautiful.

"You did all this for me?" she asks. The villagers nod and smile proudly.

Mrs Rainbow sits staring at the patchwork of colour until darkness falls. She reluctantly makes her way indoors feeling very happy indeed.

Several days later, the District Councillors return to the cottage with another important letter for Mrs Rainbow to read:

The District Council
Planning Office,
Greyfriars Road,
Blackford.
Co. Dullham.

To Mrs Rainbow

At our recent monthly planning meeting, it was decided unanimously that your un-named house is not in keeping with the rest of the village.

It was agreed that your cottage is far too dull and should be painted in the brightest colours immediately.

Signed: The District Council
Planning Committee

Mrs Rainbow can hardly contain her excitement and hugs each of the councillors, (much to their embarrassment) before rushing into the village to tell everyone the wonderful news. After a visit to Fred Stanley's DIY Store, she invites the whole village to a 'Painting Party' to thank them for their kindness.

The cottage is soon restored to its original beauty …

… and that afternoon the villagers enjoy a delicious and colourful afternoon tea.

The party is briefly interrupted by a sudden change in the weather as a summer shower forces everyone to rush inside.

However, on their return to the garden they are treated to a beautiful surprise.

As Mrs Rainbow admires the colourful scene, she notices that not only the weather is changing!

Other books by
Neil Griffiths:

Grandma Brown's Three Fine Pigs	ISBN 0-9537099-7-3
If Only	ISBN 0-9540498-4-5
If Only *(In Welsh)*	ISBN 0-9540498-6-1
Itchy Bear	ISBN 0-9540498-1-0
Itchy Bear *(Big book)*	ISBN 0-9540498-3-7
Messy Martin	ISBN 0-9545353-4-0
No room for a baby roo!	ISBN 0-9545353-8-3
Ringo The Flamingo	ISBN 0-9540498-2-9
The Journey	ISBN 0-9545353-6-7
The Journey *(Big book)*	ISBN 0-9537099-6-5
The Scarecrow Who Didn't Scare	ISBN 0-9540498-0-2
Walter's Windy Washing Line	ISBN 0-9545353-0-8
Walter's Windy Washing Line *(Big book)*	ISBN 0-9545353-1-6
Who'd be a fly?	ISBN 0-9545353-5-9